MAY   1995

qJ ρ

Pilkey, Dav, 1966-

The Moonglow Roll-a-Rama

5/31/95
3/25/14
㊷
1 owner

The MOONGLOW Roll-O-Rama

by

Dav Pilkey

ORCHARD BOOKS • NEW YORK

To Carolyn
and her three skaters,
Oscar, Rosie, and Josephine

Orchard Books, 95 Madison Avenue, New York, NY 10016

Manufactured in the United States of America
Printed by Barton Press, Inc. Bound by Horowitz/Rae.
Book design by Mina Greenstein
The text of this book is set in 18 point Kabel Demibold.
The illustrations are watercolor with pencil, reproduced in full color.
1 3 5 7 9 10 8 6 4 2

Library of Congress Cataloging-in-Publication Data
Pilkey, Dav, date. The Moonglow Roll-O-Rama / by Dav Pilkey.
p.   cm. "A Richard Jackson book"—Half t.p.
Summary: At night when the light of the moon is aglow,
animals skate at a magical roller rink.
ISBN 0-531-06876-5.   ISBN 0-531-08726-3 (lib. bdg.)
[1. Animals—Fiction. 2. Roller skating—Fiction.
3. Night—Fiction. 4. Stories in rhyme.]   I. Title.
PZ8.3.P55867Mo   1995   [E]—dc20   94-24846

Have you ever wondered
Where animals go,
At night when the light
Of the moon is aglow?

When dusk is upon them
And shadows are growing,
Just *where* are all of
Those animals going?

Why are they, *why* are they
Far away creeping,
While all of the rest
Of the world is asleeping?

And how come the creatures
Away in the zoo
Escape from their cages
And come along, too?

Journeying, journeying
Through the deep trees,
Across the wet rivers
And over the seas.

Away to an island
    Beyond a lagoon,
Below the tall treetops
    Beneath a blue moon . . .

There lies in a clearing
    A glorious sight:
The Moonglow Roll-O-Rama . . .
    (And it's open all night!)

And there all the creatures
Together are drawn
To sitting and fitting
Their rollin' shoes on.

They string up their laces
And head for the floor,
Leaving collars and leashes
Behind at the door.

From the biggest of bigs,
To the smallest of smalls.

The animals skate—
And nobody falls.

There's magic in moonlight—
    The creatures detect it.
It finds them each night
    For they merely expect it.

The magic sweeps all of them
Over the sky,
To moonglow enchanted
Where animals fly.

Skating in moonlight
    And drifting in breezes,
Rolling in starshine
    And dancing in treeses . . .

Up up they go
    Through star-riddled haze,
Those animals skating
    Celestial ballets.

They say it gets darkest
   Just before dawn,
The clouds rolling in
   And the moonlight is gone.

And magic begins to wear off
   All around.
And animals make their way
   Back to the ground.

Skating and hoping
That night never ends,
Paw-in-paw, hoof-in-claw,
Animal Friends.

Now hurrying hurrying
As the dawn breaks,
Those creatures are scurrying
Out of their skates

And back through the morning
They dash and they leap,
Away to their pillows
To slumber and sleep.

So now you know why
    All day they are sleeping.
And now you know where
    At night they are creeping.

Animals, animals
  Dreaming of when
They'll meet in the Moonglow . . .

And go skating again.